The Midnight Ride of Blackwell Station

The Midnight Ride of Blackwell Station

Written by Mary Peace Finley

Illustrated by Judith Hunt

To David, my grandson

ISBN: 978-0-86541-106-7
Library of Congress Control Number: 2010926600
Copyright © 2010 Mary Peace Finley
ALL RIGHTS RESERVED

Cover and interior art copyright © 2010 Judith Hunt
Book design by Beth Kooima

P.O. Box 95 • Palmer Lake, CO 80133
888-570-2663
FilterPressBooks.com

Printed in the United States of America on acid free paper.

The Middle of Nowhere

Raephy glanced around the bedroom, dropped to her knees, peeled back the corner of the rag rug beside the bed, and pressed her eye to the knothole. In the train station below, her mother was sorting mail on the large desk that held a coil of wire, a telegraph key and a telegraphic sounder. Outside, Raephy could hear her older brother Harry and their Daddy fixing broken boards on the cattle chutes. Abruptly the sounder clicked into action, its sound amplified by the empty Prince Albert tobacco can behind it.

Raephy squinted through the knothole, trying to read the words that zipped across the page from her mother's pen. *Dit-dit*—That was "I". *Dah-dit*—That was "N" "In…." something. Then she was lost. How could Mama remember all those letters?

She turned her head, surprised to see the toes of her little sister's bare feet wiggling beside her nose. "We're in luck, Sadie!" Raephy flipped the rug back over the knothole and jumped up. "If we ask Mama now, she'll let us go play. A telegram's coming in. She's too busy to say no."

Raephy and Sadie tiptoed past the curtain between their room and the kitchen area where their big sister Laura was kneading bread dough. Then they rumbled down the stairs into the station. "Mama, may we…"

"Shhhh!" Their mother waved them toward the door. "Be back before the next train," she called after them as the *click-clacking* stopped. "Put on your shoes. Don't forget the razor. Make sure the blade is folded in good and tight."

From a nail by the station door, Raephy unhooked a straight edge razor on a string and hung it around her neck. Raephy held up her pinky, and Sadie linked it with hers. Freedom! At least until time for the next train and the next round of chores and lessons.

Outside, sunlight peeked through the clouds, reflecting off the last melting snowdrifts. Raephy held her hand to shade her eyes and whistled. Except for the glaring white snow, everything was brown—brown dirt, brown corrals, brown cattle, brown prairie, even the distant trees by the river were brown.

With a happy "Urf!", a patch of brown separated from the rest, and their dog Jinx bounded toward them, scooping a stick into his mouth, his brown eyes begging. "All right, Jinx. Go get it!" Raephy tossed the wet stick toward a rock. "Oops!" The rock moved. "Sorry." The rock was Harry's pet turtle.

"What shall we do, Sadie? Hunt arrowheads? Make mud pies?"

Before Sadie could answer, hoof beats thundered toward them. "Ohhh, no!" Raephy moaned. "It's Mr. Black, and does he ever look mad."

"Mr. Black always looks mad." Sadie's fingers gripped Raephy's skirt.

Jinx dropped the stick at Raephy's feet, planted his front paws and leaned forward, eyes fixed. Raephy signaled "stop!" to remind him not to growl.

Mr. Black reigned up in front of them, yanking

on the bit. Foam flicked from the corners of his horse's mouth. The horse's eyes showed white. Mr. Black hiked up the six-shooter at his side and glared down at Raephy. "Which one are you?" he grumbled.

"I'm Raephy, Mr. Black, sir."

"Where's your Pa and that worthless brother of yours?"

"Daddy and Harry are fixing the loading chutes." Raephy pointed beyond the station to the two figures working between the train tracks and the corrals.

"McDowell!" Black bellowed, spurring his horse. "McDowell! Texans are driving longhorns onto my ranch." Without a thank-you, he galloped away, showering Raephy and Sadie with gravel and dirt.

"Poor horse," Sadie murmured, letting Raephy's skirt hang free.

"Poor Texans." Raephy scratched behind Jinx's ear. "All they want is to load their cattle into cattle cars. Isn't that what Blackwell Station's for? Cattle? It sure isn't for kids!"

When Daddy told them a train station was being named for their family, Raephy was excited. "Black" for the rancher, Mr. Black, and "well" for Daddy, John

"Where's your Pa and that worthless brother of yours?"

Alexander McDowell, the ranch foreman. None of their family or friends back in Pennsylvania had train stations named after them. It seemed so special—then. "But now—"

"Now what, Raephy?"

Had she said that out loud?

"Sadie," Raephy sighed, "don't you miss living in a town with schools and churches and stores and friends to play with? A place where we wouldn't have to wear razors in case we get bitten by a rattlesnake? I don't ever want to cut an *X* over fang holes and suck out the poison. Eeuuuu!"

Just then their father and Mr. Black galloped by. Harry trailed, behind riding Sugar, his little mare. "Raephy!" he shouted. "If you want your book, it's on my bunk in the shed. Tell Mother we'll be late."

Raephy didn't want to frighten Sadie, so she called out to Harry and Daddy only with her mind: *Be careful, Harry. Be safe, Daddy. Those Texans will be as angry as Mr. Black, and they'll be wearing six-shooters, too.*

Raephy looked around at the endless flat prairie and the long straight line of railroad tracks. Mr. Black's house was the only other house for as far as she could see, but her house—the McDowell house—wasn't really a house at all. It was only two small rooms on the second floor of a rickety train station smack in the middle of nowhere. Blackwell Station.

Dah-dah-dah Dit-dit-dit

Raephy swept the last pile of sand and weeds into a dustpan then looked around the one big room of Blackwell Station. In the alcove where Mama worked, everything was tidy, in its place. Papers and mail were neatly stacked and weighted down to keep the strong gusts of wind that swooped through the station from carrying them away.

Mama's telegraph office was a three-sided bay window extending out from the station. The windows looked out on the tracks in three directions so the telegraph operator could see trains arriving, unloading and departing. Raephy reached over the desk to wipe a smudge from the windowpane then straightened the sign that hung above the telegraph equipment. For about the millionth time read the words:

Is it not a feat sublime?
Intellect has conquered time.

Then she drew a neat black *X* through yesterday's date on the wall calendar—April 14, 1886.

She listened for the telegraph as she worked. Even though she couldn't keep up with every *dah* and *dit*, she helped Mama by receiving and sending the most common message, "On Schedule." O.S. for short. *Dah-dah-dah Dit-dit-dit,* plus the station name, train number and direction the train was traveling. Easy.

Bong! The wall clock chimed the half hour, and Jinx poked his head in the door. "Urf?"

"Jinx." Raephy shook her head. "You know you're not allowed inside." She crossed to the doorway, sat down, and rubbed her forehead against his. "Have you been chasing the cats again?" She touched a new scratch on his nose.

Jinx lowered his head and looked up the way Granddad looked at her over the top of his eyeglasses.

Overhead, a chamber pot scraped across the floor. Raephy's nose wrinkled, even though she couldn't smell it. That was one of her big sister Laura's jobs—emptying and washing chamber pots every morning and cleaning the outhouse and cooking and baking and washing and ironing and watching Sadie and helping with lessons and taking over for Mama in the telegraph alcove.

"Poor Laura." Raephy sighed. "Is that why she seems so unhappy, Jinx? Because she has to act grown-up all the time and doesn't get to go to school or have any friends?"

Jinx cocked his ear, *eerfed*, then bounded toward the sound of Harry's harmonica out by the corral.

Raephy stood, brushed dirt from her skirt and went back inside. She flipped her dust rag over the black potbelly stove. For several days the early spring weather had been warm enough not to need a fire, and there weren't any ashes to clean out of the ash box. Her chores were almost finished.

Breakfast had been over for a long time, but Mama was bustling around upstairs in the kitchen. The warm sweet scents of something delicious that drifted down the stairwell made Raephy hungry all over again. "Smells good, doesn't it, Mr. William Barstow Strong?" She ran her dust cloth around the black and white drawing of the president of the Atchison, Topeka, and Santa Fe Railway. *Dah-dah-dah dit-dit-dit.* The sounder rattled. Raephy grabbed a pencil and wrote, "O. S."

"The next eastbound train is on schedule, Mr. Lincoln," she said, shaking dust from the faded black cloth draped above President Lincoln's photograph. Beneath the photograph were the dates: February 12, 1809 – April 15, 1865. "Oh!" she said aloud, glancing back at the calendar. "Today is April 15, too! It's been twenty-one years." She wished she could reach into the picture to smooth his rumpled hair and straighten his bow tie and tell him how sorry she was.

"Raephy, are you talking to Lincoln again?" Laughing, her daddy stepped over the threshold, and his boot thumped on the wooden floor.

"Daddy!" Raephy ran into his open arms for his big bear hug. It wasn't Sunday, but he was wearing a clean shirt, a brand new pair of denim waist overalls, and his white Stetson hat. He smelled of sage-scented yucca soap. Just last week, she and Laura had made that soap in a big three-legged black kettle behind the station.

Daddy swung her in a circle until her feet lifted off the floor and the dust rag fluttered like a handkerchief. "Maybe I should be talking to Lincoln, too." Daddy said. "I could use some advice from a great diplomat this morning."

Raephy's feet found the floor and Daddy's voice took on a serious tone. "Listen, Raephy." His eyes scanned the room. "The Railroad Superintendent, Mr. Marshall, is coming this morning. Have you been OS–ing the trains? Will he be on time?"

"Yes. Dah-dah-dah. Dit-dit-dit." Raephy tapped the message on her Daddy's arm. "The train's O.S."

"Now, Raephy, you make yourself scarce when Mr. Marshall gets here. Understood?"

'Scarce' Raephy understood, but Daddy hadn't exactly told her to go away, had he? Why was he so serious? Last night she'd heard Mama and Daddy talking softly about Mr. Black and the Texas cattlemen when they thought everyone else was asleep. "Amos is stuck in his ways," she'd heard Daddy say. "He's not going to change his mind."

Was that why Mr. Marshall was coming?

Sweeping the station platform took an unusually long time this morning, and Raephy didn't finish until the next train came huffing into the station, pulling a passenger car. She hopped off the platform, knelt, reached underneath with the broom to chase away any spiders and crawled into the dark space striped with sunlight. She wouldn't be able to see anyone from under here, but she would hear everything. She was "scarce" enough, wasn't she?

The train wheezed and clanked to a stop.

"Morning, Mr. Marshall," Daddy's voice said. "Welcome to Blackwell Station."

"Good morning, John." *Thump. Thump. Thump.* Mr. Marshall's feet echoed across the platform. "Beautiful day. It's about time after all those horrible blizzards this winter."

Swish. Swish. Softer footsteps. "Good morning, Mr. Marshall." Mama pronounced every syllable as if she were giving a spelling lesson.

"Ahhhh! Good morning, Emily! Fine job you're doing with this station, ma'am. I appreciate it. Black isn't here yet?"

"He should be here soon," Mama said, "Shall we go in? I've made coffee and chokecherry scones."

Feet pounded overhead. Dirt filtered down through the cracks onto Raephy's face into her eyes. Blinking, she scrambled out from under the platform and brushed grit from her knees and elbows and spider webs from her eyelashes. She was crawling across the platform beneath the bay window when Jinx poked the back of her skirt with his cold nose.

"Eeep! Jinx!" She clamped her hand around his muzzle. "Quiet!" She scrunched down cross-legged under an window where Mama and Daddy and Mr. Marshall wouldn't see her. "Lie down!" she whispered, pulling Jinx's head onto her lap.

"Just as well Black's not here yet," Mr. Marshall said. "I'm glad for the chance to talk with you in private." A cup clicked against a saucer. "Mmm! These scones are delicious!"

"I'm glad you like them, Mr. Marshall."

"Oh, please, Emily! Call me Ed. Both of you. Call me Ed." He paused. "Now, John, I know you're the foreman of Black's ranch, and I understand you've claimed a homestead to prove up for him. But let's set that aside for a minute."

"All right." Daddy sounded hesitant. "But about those Texans, I've already talked with Amos. He's a stubborn man, Amos is, against change. He wants only local ranchers to load cattle here. He's not going to let Texas drovers cross his land."

Mr. Marshall waved his hand as if to brush away a fly. "Listen John, Emily, I haven't come just to talk about cattle. Something bigger is coming down the track. Something that will help more people than Black's cattle empire ever could."

Raephy pushed Jinx off her lap, rolled onto her knees, and stretched to see over the windowsill. What was this superintendent talking about?

"Now, John and Emily, you know that because of the railroad many homesteaders have come here to settle. More are arriving all the time." Mr. Marshall looked up at Lincoln's photograph—"Thanks to Lincoln's land grant bill, the railroad owns land on both sides of the tracks and larger plots for settlements and farms. We need schools and land offices and churches for all these new people. And a doctor and a dentist and…We need a town, John. And one of these days, a county seat."

A town? A town! Raephy could hardly choke her heart back down into her chest.

"You know, of course, that this station, the corrals—none of this—belongs to Black. It all belongs to the railroad. Emily, you're already in the employ of the Santa Fe Railway. And the Atchison, Topeka, and Santa Fe would be generous in showing its appreciation to the both of you, and your children, and their children, if you can help convince Amos Black to sell us land for a town site."

"Oh, my!" Mama exclaimed. "Oh! Wouldn't that be wonderful?"

"It would, indeed." Mr. Marshall nodded. "The station is already here. Last year, Ol' Buffalo Jones cleared off what was left of the buffalo. This is the perfect location for a new town. Absolutely perfect!"

"Here!" Raephy screamed, shooting up off her feet like a bucking bronco. "Right here, at Blackwell Station?"

Her mother stormed out onto the platform. "Why, Raephy McDowell! You little spy. You have no business being here. Go out to the corral and stay there until I come for you. And don't repeat a word of what you've heard. Not a word!"

Raephy scrunched down cross-legged under a window where Mama and Daddy and Mr. Marshall wouldn't see her.

Raephy ran. But she could have been turning somersaults through the cow pies. A town! A town! Right here. Schools and churches and a store! And kids and fireworks and birthday parties and balloons and music and dances.

Moments later, Mr. Amos Black rode in and looped his horse's reins over a hitching rail. The reins were still swinging when he stomped back out of the station yelling. Raephy could hear him just fine, even from the corral.

"No! No! No! This is cattle country. I will not sell an inch of my land for a town. Towns and cattle don't mix. You know that. Settlers. Homesteaders. Roads. Fences. Farms. Ditches. Canals. They'd ruin the prairies for grazing."

He thumped across the platform, unhitched the reins, and swung himself up into the saddle. "No! No Texans. No town. No platters. No boomers. And that's final!"

Mr. Tall Man

Raephy didn't say a word to anyone, not even to Sadie or Laura. But then, there was nothing to say. It was as if Mr. Marshall had given her a big slice of rich chocolate cake with creamy fudge frosting, then snatched it away before she could take a single bite.

Her parents had never been so angry with her, never in her whole nine years. After Mr. Marshall left, Mama stomped a straight line to the corral. "Raephy! You know better than to stick your nose into other people's business. Don't ever do that again!"

But Raephy argued. "Isn't what happens at Blackwell Station my business? Don't I live here, too?"

"Well, yes. I suppose it is, but some business simply isn't meant for little ears. Daddy and I will tell you what you need to know when the time is right."

A week later her mother's scolding voice still spread like a bruise on her memory, and Raephy was still doing extra chores and going to bed early without dessert. "Penance" Mama called it. Raephy called it just plain mean.

Laura must have agreed. One night while the family was eating dessert without her, Laura whispered "Shhhh!" and slipped a dish of rice pudding under the curtain.

In the weeks that followed Mr. Marshall's visit, through the rest of April and the first twelve days of May, Raephy didn't hear another word about a new town. Then late one night, Mama and Daddy tip-toed downstairs. They didn't go outside to talk the way they had since Mr. Marshall came, so even though she knew better, Raephy slipped quietly from beneath the stack of quilts and pressed her eye, then her ear to the knothole. At first, their whispers were too quiet to hear, but then Mama's voice rose. "…this shack! Not even enough room for Harry to sleep…" Her voice faded, then rose again,

"...wind and snow...right through the cracks in these flimsy walls...so isolated! John, this is not the best place to raise our children."

"Emily, Emily, Shush!"

Mama shushed, but Raephy could still hear every word. "You *must* persuade Amos Black to reconsider and if you can't—" Mama's chair squealed as she jumped to her feet. "The Santa Fe wants a town and I do, too. As an employee of the Santa Fe, and as the mother of our children, I want you to know, John Alexander McDowell, that I will do everything I can to help make that happen!" Mama grabbed the lantern and charged up the stairs. "Good night."

Fast as a snake Raephy slithered back under the quilts, eyes wide open, hardly able to believe her ears. Whenever Mama called any of them by all three names, they knew they were in big trouble, but this time, it wasn't one of the kids. Were Mama and Daddy arguing? Fighting? Were they at war with each other?

Mama's words replayed inside Raephy's head as loudly as the noises around her. Sister Sadie sprawled like an eagle across the middle of the bed making funny little chirpy sounds through her nose. Laura stretched straight as a pin along the opposite edge, mumbling to a sweetheart who lived only in her dreams.

Raephy didn't know how they could sleep at all because spring roundup was in full swing. Outside, cattle bumped and bawled and bellowed in the sorting pens and corrals. Hooves drummed the hollow-sounded wooden floors of the cattle cars. The cattle were louder than ten thunderstorms, louder than twenty train engines, louder than…Raephy twisted and turned and turned and twisted and finally covered her head with a pillow to muffle the noise. But she couldn't stop hearing over and over again Mama's words inside her head.

Sometime during the night she must have gone to sleep. Suddenly it was morning and Sadie was tugging her arm. "Raephy! You're going to miss breakfast. Get up! Mama needs you."

Raephy dragged herself out of bed, shivered into her clothes, and tried to pull a comb through the knots in her hair. She shuffled through the opening in the curtain into the other room crowded with Mama and Daddy's bed, the cookstove, a small table, two chairs, two orange crates they used for stools, and six people.

"Raephy?" Mama frowned. "Do you feel all right?"

Her soft hand brushed Raephy's cheek.

"Uh-huh." Cattle were still bawling as Raephy flopped into her place on the edge of the bed.

"There will be more trains than usual today. I need your help in the station," Mama said, squeezing past Raephy's knees. "Laura dear, give Raephy a new list of spelling words to work on downstairs. And see what you can do with her hair. It looks like a tangle of rusty barbed wire."

"Can I telegraph with Raephy?"

"Not today, Sadie bunny."

Sadie pouted, but their mother was already on her way to work, her hair in a tidy bun, and her dress covered with a stiff white apron. "Talk to him, John," she called over her shoulder.

A frown rippled across Daddy's forehead and as he stood, he sighed. "We'd better go, Harry. Get to work, girls."

Laura cleared Raephy's oatmeal bowl from the table. Then she filled a page with numbers, another page with words, and handed them to Raephy.

"I already know how to spell these," Raephy grumbled, squinting at the blurry pencil marks.

"Really?" Laura cocked her head to one side. "How do you spell hippopotamus?" She nodded as Raephy sleepily drawled out the letters. "And how do you spell the plural?"

"H-i-p-p-o-p-o-t-a-m-u-s-s-e-s?'"

"H-i-p-p-o-p-o-t-a-m-i."

"Who cares?" Raephy mumbled.

"You do, Raephy. You know you do. Telegraphers must be good spellers."

"Nobody is going to telegraph Blackwell Station about hippopotami!" Raephy snatched the papers and thumped down the stairs to the station.

Usually Raephy liked talking and listening to the railroad conductors and engineers and workers. There weren't ever many passengers, but once in a while travelers stepped out onto the platform. She liked to hear about the cities and towns they'd left behind, but today no passengers stepped down from the train. She keyed the O.S. message to the next station then went outside and sat on the edge of the platform, close enough to hear the sounder.

A few minutes later, Mama knelt beside her on the platform, stroking Jinx's head. "Are you sure you're all right, sweetie?"

Raephy nodded. "I'm just tired. The cows kept me awake all night." She wished she could ask Mama what she'd meant when she said, *I'll do everything I can to see that happen!*

"Why don't you get one of your books and read for awhile? I'll take over at the desk now. Maybe I've been working you too hard."

Raephy was caught up in *Uncle Tom's Cabin* when the next westbound train arrived. It was Engine #345 pulling a string of empty cattle cars.

A well-dressed man in a black hat jumped down onto the platform before the train had come to a full stop. He was carrying a long roll of paper. Something interesting was afoot. Raephy set *Uncle Tom's Cabin* on the platform, wiped her nose, and glanced at her reflection in the bay window to check her hair.

"Hello!" she called out over the screech of train wheels. "Welcome to Blackwell Station. My name's Raephy. Raephy Mc-Dow-WELL...like the station." She stuck out her hand. "What's your name?"

But the tall man was already walking quickly inside. Raephy followed.

Mr. Tall-Man-In-A-Black-Hat waited until her mother finished keying the O.S. message over the wire, then he raised the long roll of paper, waving it like a flag of victory. "Emily, we got it! I've just returned from Washington, and we got it! Keep this in the safe. Watch for an important telegram a week from Saturday."

"From?"

"Emily, believe me. The less you know about the details, the better. Just make sure *you*—not one of your children—are at your desk on Saturday. I'll be back with the train on Sunday." He dashed out, jumped on the train, and with a toot, Engine #345 steamed away.

"Mama!" Raephy danced to her side, reaching for the paper. "What is this?"

Mrs. McDowell held up one finger. "Not a word, Raephy. Not a single word." She sang a little ditty Raephy had never heard her sing before.

Little eyes see
Little ears hear
Little tongues give secrets away.

Then Mama whispered, "It's better that you don't know."

Only a few boxes of supplies and a bag of mail had been tossed from that train, and no cattle were loaded, but Raephy swept the platform again, very slowly so she could hear over the swish-swish of the bristles. Something mysterious was happening. Her mother knew what it was, and Raephy wanted to know, too, but all she heard after the safe door thumped closed was the *clickety-clack-clack* of the telegraph and the *tick-tock* of the clock.

The Handcar

That long roll of paper locked in the safe teased Raephy's mind night and day. Nine *X*s on the calendar later, she was still trying to imagine what it could be. She would know soon. Day after tomorrow, Sunday, the Tall Man said he would return.

"Engine #345!" Raephy exclaimed as the next train pulled into Blackwell Station. "That's my lucky engine, Sadie!" Engine #345 was beginning to feel like an old friend. And sure enough, the two men who stepped onto the platform were every bit as interesting as Mr. Tall-Man-In-A-Black-Hat.

"Well, well, well!" said the older man who

was round like a potato and wore a pretty vest with a golden chain draped between pockets. "You must be the McDowell girls! Let's see." He squinted down. "Raephy? And Sadie! Am I right?"

For once, Raephy was at a loss for words. She could only nod.

"And this," he fished a piece of hard tack from one of the many pockets over his belly, "must be Jinx."

"Urf?" Jinx hunkered down on his front legs, tail wagging, then with a *clack!* caught the dry biscuit between his teeth.

"Now, Mr. Ament," the potato-shaped man said, nodding to the young man beside him, "with beautiful girls like these already here, how could you go wrong?"

"We have an older sister, too!" Raephy said. "Laura. She's the pretty one."

The young man smiled, but his face had turned a strange shade of red. "It's a fine location, Captain Cooper." His eyes scanned the prairie around the station. "But where's it going to be?"

"Oh, not here! On about three, four miles, but the train—. Well, the train won't go, err, doesn't go, doesn't stop there. Not yet. Not until Sunday."

"What?" Young Mr. Ament fidgeted as if ants had crawled up inside his pants legs. "But I've come all the way from Topeka! I'm not stopping now."

Captain Cooper dabbed his rosy cheeks with the large white handkerchief he pulled from another of his many pockets. "Having a look ahead of time is a splendid idea, Mr. Ament. I assure you, you won't be sorry, but it'd be a mighty long walk. I'll tell you what..." He was eyeing the handcar that two railroad workers were pumping along newly-laid tracks.

Before Raephy knew it, before Mama had even come out to say hello, Captain Cooper and young Mr. Ament had crossed the tracks, said something to the workers, climbed aboard the little flatbed of the handcar, and were pumping their way into the sunset.

"Well, I never!" Raephy said. It was the first time in her life she'd ever said that.

"Well, I never!" Sadie echoed.

"Well, I never!" Behind them, in the doorway, Mama laughed. "I never thought I'd see a high-falutin' associate of the Santa Fe Land Company like Captain Cooper pumping a handcar!"

"Where are they going, Mama?"

Mama's eyes twinkled, her shoulders raised, her hands opened, palms up, and she shrugged the biggest fake shrug Raephy had ever seen.

The Telegram

Raephy heard Mama and Daddy coming toward the station and scrambled for cover before she saw them, but spying from inside the one room of Blackwell Station was practically impossible. The straight wooden benches along the walls wouldn't hide anyone. She didn't have time to crawl under Mama's desk or run upstairs to the knothole or outside under the bay window.

The only thing Raephy could do when the clock struck three and Mama and Daddy rushed in, was to hide behind the potbelly stove. She hunkered down, spread her legs wide, bent her knees, and scooted one foot, then the other, directly behind the stove's black legs. To keep from losing her balance, she clamped her arms around the curves on the back of the stove's big round belly. Like hugging Captain Cooper, she thought.

Daddy almost never came to the station with Mama, but here he was. Something out of the ordinary was definitely about to happen. Raephy was sure it must have something to do with the tall man and the long roll of paper and a telegram. Even though Raephy knew she shouldn't be listening, she had to know what.

Mama's desk chair squeaked, and Daddy's feet scuffed back and forth across the wooden floor. "When's the telegram going to come in?" Daddy sounded angry, but Raephy knew he was just impatient, as impatient as she was.

"I don't know, dear. He just said that an important telegram would arrive today, and that he'd be back tomorrow. It could come any minute now."

As if on cue, the sounder clicked into action *Dit-dah dah-dah dah-dah-dah dit-dit-dit.*

Deciphering Morse Code that quickly made Raephy's head feel as if it would explode. *Dit-dah.* That meant A. *Dah-dah* meant M. *Dah-dah-dah* = O. *Dit-dit-dit* = S. The sounder paused and Mama's pen scratched

The only thing Raephy could do when Mama and Daddy rushed in, was hide behind the potbelly stove.

the first word on the paper. Raephy strung the letters together in her head: A-m-o-s, Amos. The first word was Amos. The sounder clicked into action again. *Dah-dit-dit-dit* = B. *dit-dah-dit-dit* = L. Bl…Black. The telegram was for Amos Black.

Raephy's leg muscles started to quiver. Her nose itched. The kink in her neck twitched. Slowly she turned her head, pressed her nose and forehead against the cool cast iron, reached out just a little ways farther around the potbelly, and hugged even harder to give her legs a rest. The sounder stopped.

"Amos Black," Mama read aloud. "Urgent business. Take next train to Pueblo."

Daddy laughed. "Well! If that doesn't get him away from here, I don't know what will." He slapped his leg. "This is going to work! Unless someone's spilled the beans. Uhh, where's Raephy?"

Raephy's leg muscles turned to pudding. She hugged Captain Cooper even harder, gripping cast iron with her fingernails to keep from sliding down onto the floor.

At first she thought the sounds she heard were laughter, but then realized they were coughs, one high and one low, followed by a long, long, very long silence.

"Well, Emily, she may be a good spy, but she sure wouldn't make a good poker player," Daddy said. "She's showing her hand."

Mama giggled just as Raephy's legs gave out.

"Raephy McDowell, you are incorrigible!" Mama leaned over her, shaking a finger, but Raephy could see that her mother was trying hard not to laugh. "I thought you learned your lesson about spying."

"Lucky you didn't pull the stove over on you!" Daddy scooped Raephy up, carried her dangling between his hands, and plopped her down on Mama's chair. "So, Little Miss Spy, I suppose you heard all of that." His face was so close to her nose that Raephy could see curlicues in his whiskers and smell something like alfalfa on his breath. She nodded and bowed her head, studying a fish-shaped scratch on her arm.

"Raephy," Mama asked, "have you said anything, anything at all about the man who came with the roll of paper?"

"No, Mama." Raephy traced the fish design with a ragged fingernail.

"Or about Captain Cooper riding away on the handcar?"

"No, Mama."

"Not to anyone? Not to Mr. Black or any of his cowhands?"

"No."

"We know how much you like to talk with people, Raephy, and

Little ears hear.

Little eyes see.

Little tongues give secrets away."

There was such a long pause that finally Raephy couldn't stand the silence any longer. She jumped out of the chair, planted her fists on her hips, and narrowed her eyes the way Jinx did when he looked at Mr. Black. "I. Haven't. Told. Anyone. Anything!"

Mama breathed in a deep breath and sighed. "All right, then."

"A lot is at stake here today, Raephy," Daddy said. "Since we can't seem to keep anything from you, you better stay right here with us. You can listen, but don't interrupt, and wipe that soot off your nose."

Daddy thumped the telegram on the desk with a strong finger, then looked up at the big clock on the wall.

"It's time to get this message to Amos."

"Which of us will take it?" Mama asked. "When he figures out what's happened, he'll be suspicious. He'll think the messenger is in on it."

Daddy rubbed the back of his neck. "If I take it he'll be suspicious even sooner."

"My job, then," Mama said, picking up the message.

"I could take it," Raephy squeaked.

"Don't interrupt!" Mama spun toward Raephy.

"But I could take it. He wouldn't suspect me," Raephy repeated softly, scrunching down in the chair.

"Emily, wait. Raephy has a good idea."

"No!" Mama shook her head so hard the bun in her hair tumbled loose.

"Yes," Daddy insisted. "You've received a telegram the way you always do, and you've simply asked Raephy to deliver the message."

Mama sighed again, then she smiled. "Well then, Raephy, I guess it's the price you pay for being a spy."

She tried to arrange her hair back onto the top of her head. "You're not afraid of Mr. Black, are you?"

"Not much. He doesn't even know my name. I'll take Jinx. He'll protect me."

"Now, Raephy, no matter what happens, you must not say anything to any of the ranch hands or give the message to anyone but Mr. Black. And you must find him. This is very important."

Mama held up the telegram. "Now hurry. Take this to Mr. Black so he can get ready to leave. Then skedaddle right back home, find Harry, and come inside."

Raephy grabbed the piece of paper and raced out the door. Mysteriously, all the cattle had been loaded and shipped away. Only the horses remained, and the corrals were so quiet Raephy could hear meadowlarks singing.

"Come on, Jinx." She snapped her fingers, and Jinx bounded away from the back step. "We're on an important mission."

Raephy and Jinx ran all the way to Mr. Black's ranch house and spotted him out back, grooming his horse. "Guess he's not always mean to that poor horse," Raephy said, scratching Jinx's ear while she caught her breath.

"Mr. Black," she called out, holding up the message. "This telegram's for you."

"Well, bring it over here, girl." Mr. Black tossed the brush onto the ground. "Which one are you, anyhow?"

"I'm Raephy, Mr. Black, sir."

"Much obliged, Raephy," he said, tipping his hat. "Thank you."

"You're welcome, Mr. Black," she said and turned and ran like the wind.

Dressed to the Nines

Unless it was for breakfast or the noon meal, the McDowell family seldom gathered during the day. Everyone was too busy with work or lessons, but after Raephy delivered the message to Mr. Black, she followed the sound of Harry's harmonica and herded him upstairs just as Mama had asked.

"Harry!" Sadie jumped up from the kitchen table where she was coloring. "Look what I drew?"

Laura turned away from the dishpan, wet hands dripping like puppy paws. "What are you doing back here at this time of day?"

"Yeah," Harry said, his voice lower than it really was. "What are we all doing here?"

41

"Your mother will tell us." As soon as the *clickety-clack* of the telegraph stopped, Daddy called downstairs. "Coming, Emily?"

Mama's footsteps pattered up the stairs and she glided into the kitchen. Her stiff white apron was off-kilter, high on one side, low on the other. Her cheeks were as rosy as if she'd stayed in the sun all morning. "All right, then!" she said breathlessly. "Everyone's here."

She looked at Daddy, then took a deep breath. "We're going to be doing things differently this afternoon, so pay attention. First of all, don't anyone go wandering off. Next, it's Saturday, bath night, but we'll take our baths early. Harry, start carrying up the bath water for Laura to heat."

"But Dad and I still have to check fences."

"Emily, couldn't we skip the baths this week?" Daddy asked. "We have a lot to do."

Mama shook her head so hard that sprigs of hair popped out of her bun. Like rusty barbed wire, Raephy thought. "We might not be settled enough for baths by next Saturday, John," Mama said, half under her breath.

"Well, son," Daddy shrugged, "looks like we won't

be checking fences. Do as your mother says."

Mama was fluttering around the kitchen like a trapped house swallow. "Laura, dear, I want you to milk the cow."

"But I milked Bessie this morning."

"Milk her again, and don't give her any more hay. Bring the clothes in from the clothesline on your way back...and bring the clothespins, too. Then watch the telegraph for me."

"Sadie bunny, I need you to take the basket and see if the hens have laid any more eggs." She ran her hand down Sadie's braid. "What about the chickens, John?"

"We'll take care of them after the train leaves."

"Now, listen carefully, all of you. You'll know what this is all about soon enough, but for now, do as I've asked. And tonight —" She shrugged. "Tonight—well, just use your heads. Raephy, I need you to help me pack the breakables."

"Pack! Why?" Raephy asked.

"Never you mind."

When the next westbound train pulled in, Mama was reaching down from a step ladder handing dishes to Raephy.

Raephy looked out the window. "Look, Mama! There goes Mr. Black, all dressed to the nines."

Mama only smiled.

By the Light of the Gibbous Moon

Raephy's eyes popped open. Even with a slice missing from its right side, the gibbous moon shone through the window casting a shaft of bright light into her eyes.

She didn't know when Daddy and Harry had stopped hammering out by the chicken coop, but now the night was so quiet it was almost scary. Quiet, but not calm, as if the house and the station below were holding their breath.

Chuff!

Raephy bolted straight up in bed.

Chuff! Chuff! Chuff!

She rubbed her eyes. A train? In the middle of the night? With no whistle?

The big clock downstairs struck. *Bong! Bong! Bong! Bong! Bong! Bong! Bong! Bong! Bong! Bong! Bong! Bong!* Twelve! A train at midnight? Raephy dropped to her knees and peeked through the knothole at the top of Mama's head. An oil lamp with a yellow flame flickered on the desk, and Mama was sitting in her chair, fully dressed, tapping out a message.

"Daddy!" Raephy raced behind the curtain into the other room. "Daddy, there's a train! Daddy?" But Daddy wasn't there. The bed hadn't been slept in.

She ducked back into the girls' room. "Yipes!" Raephy stopped short. At the window, Laura's and Sadie's white nightgowns shimmered like ghosts in the moonlight. "You scared me!" she said, squeezing between them.

"I didn't think anything ever scared you," Laura said.

"Ghosts do! And ghost trains at midnight!" Raephy shivered. "But look!" She pointed at the approaching train. "Engine #345! That's my lucky engine."

Brakes screeching, Engine #345 wheezed to a stop beside the station. It was pulling two flatcars and work cars loaded with men. Lots of men! An army of attacking soldiers, they poured out of the cars and jumped down onto the platform carrying picks and shovels and hammers and jacks and blocks.

Bounding and barking, Jinx chased after one man, then another. One group of workers rushed toward the corrals. Another circled behind the station.

Another group began scratching and gnawing around the foundation, like a pack of giant rats. One man shinnied up the telegraph pole beside the train tracks and started removing the telegraph wire that ran to the station.

"What are they doing, Laura?" Cautiously, Sadie leaned out, peered to the right, then to the left.

"I wish I knew, Sadie. Let's move our bed under the window. We can keep warm under the covers while we watch." Laura tugged on the bedpost, but it wouldn't budge. "Help me," she said, but even with all three pushing, their bed wouldn't move.

Raephy dropped onto her hands and knees to investigate. "No wonder! It's bolted to the floor! Very strange!"

Pounding hammers shook the building.

"I'm scared," Sadie whimpered.

"Don't be scared." Raephy wrapped Sadie in her

arms. "Everything must be all right. Mama's downstairs at her desk. And look!" Raephy pointed. "There's the Railroad Superintendent, Mr. Marshall."

"The one with the young man on the handcar?" Quickly, Laura started brushing her hair.

"No," Raephy grumbled. "The one who made me have to do penance."

"Roll up that telegraph wire," Mr. Marshall called loudly. "Stow it away. And you fellows! Get a good grip on the platform."

Laura leaned over Raephy and Sadie, her hair crackling and sparking in the near darkness. "But maybe he's out there somewhere."

"Maybe," Raephy said.

"Ready?" Mr. Marshall yelled. "Set? Lift and pull! Pull! Pull-Pull-Pull!" Grunting, the workers slid the platform toward the rails, then hoisted the edge up onto a flatcar.

"Why did they do that?" Sadie asked.

"Shhhh!" Raephy hushed her. "Listen." Two of the workers were standing right beneath the window.

"Hard work!" one said, panting.

"Yep!" the other agreed. "But for ten dollars, dinner,

a dance, and all the beer and whiskey we can drink? I'd steal a station every night of the week."

"STEAL A STATION!" Raephy clamped her hand over her mouth. "Laura, they're stealing our station!" She poked her head out into the cool night air and looked straight down. Long pieces of wood were sticking out from under the building like logs in a campfire.

Five men carrying ropes were leading draft horses from the stock pens toward the place where the platform had stood.

"Raephy?" Laura peered through the dim light. "Isn't that Daddy and Harry?"

"They're tearing down the cattle chutes!"

Laura set her brush down on the windowsill with a thump. "But they just fixed them. What's Mr. Black going to say about that?"

"I reckon Mr. Black is going to be riled as a rooster at a cock fight about a lot of this." Raephy swept her hand across the strangely lit scene below. Little by little, all the secrets she'd overheard were beginning to make sense.

In the whitewash light of the moon, workers crawled over the corral fences and loading chutes, hammering them apart. The little shed where Harry slept was now a pile of lumber. Nothing was left of the chicken coop but another stack of wood. Next to the wood stood a row of crates and Bessie the cow.

"Hook 'em up!" Mr. Marshall called, slapping the shoulder of one of the draft horses. "The rest of you get behind the station and push."

A whip snapped, then snapped again. "Let's go. Get on there! Ho!" The draft horses snorted. The building trembled. Then it shook. Then it began to tilt to one side. "Whoooaaahhh!" Raephy yelled, grabbing Laura and Sadie as they slid across the floor. "Hold on!"

Everything But The Outhouse

Mama! Why didn't you tell us? Were you just going to leave us up there to be smashed against the walls?"

Laura stood in the yard, fists to hips facing her mother. To Raephy, Mama looked like a little girl in trouble, and Laura looked like her scolding mother.

"I'm sorry, girls," Mama said, hugging them to her. "Your daddy and I decided to let you sleep as long as you could. And Mr. Marshall was supposed to tell us *before* they started loading the station so I could get you out. But you used your heads and managed quite well, now didn't you?"

"Why didn't you tell us they were going to move the station?" Laura fumed.

Raephy patted Laura's arm. "If Mama had told us, we might have said the wrong things to the wrong people." She began to sing,

Little eyes see.

Little ears—

"Oh, hush!"

Raephy stopped singing and ducked out of the line of fire from Laura's eyes, but that jaunty tune was like a little worm in her brain. To keep from blurting it out again, she switched to another song, one she knew Laura liked. A song to make her feel better.

Did you ever hear tell of sweet Betsy from Pike,

Who crossed the wide mountains with her lover Ike,

Two yoke of cattle, and one spotted hog—

"Don't sing that, either." Laura glowered. "We'll never meet our Ikes out here in the middle of nowhere. And I don't want to end up being an old maid!"

Inch by inch the station creaked and groaned up the platform-ramp onto the flatcar. The draft horses and workmen groaned, too.

"Where are we going to live, Mama?" Sadie sniffed.

"Oh, we'll still live above the station, sweetie. The station will just be in a different place, that's all. As soon as the men have everything tied down, we can go back inside."

"And ride in the house?" Raephy guessed. "On the train? Ya-hoo!"

Mama nodded.

"In the dark?" Sadie grabbed a handful of Raephy's nightgown and twisted herself inside.

"You don't have to ride, Sadie bunny." Mama said, walking her fingers down Sadie's back. "You can hop. Or walk. It will only be three or four miles."

"But Mama! The station might fall apart!" Laura shuddered. "It could fall off."

"Once it's on the flatcar, it should be safe," Mama reassured her.

When Blackwell Station was finally sitting solidly on the flatcar, Raephy was the first to scramble on board. Singing *too-ral-i-oo-ral-i-ay*!

"Raephy!" Mr. Marshall called, reaching a lantern up to her. "Take this. Go upstairs and when we get going, watch out the window for cattle on the tracks."

Raephy felt her way along the wall. Mama, Laura and Sadie inched behind her up the dark stairway. They huddled at the window and watched the workmen load the platform onto the flatcar behind them.

Then, onto the flatcars went the boards from the corrals. On went the torn-apart cattle chutes and Harry's shed. On went the wood from the outbuildings and the water barrels and the water tank. On went the three-legged soap kettle. On went the crates of squawking chickens. Everything was loaded except Bessie and one small out building.

Raephy lit the lantern and waved it out the window. "Mr. Marshall!" she called. "You forgot the outhouse!"

Mr. Marshall chuckled. "We'll leave the outhouse for Mr. Black. He'll need it when he sees what we've done."

Finally, the train was loaded. More than loaded— overloaded! Overloaded so badly that the workers had to stand along the tracks and hold the strange cargo in place to keep it from falling off. "I'll bet they're going to have to hold the load all the way there," Raephy said.

Engine #345 fired up. Smoke billowed from the smokestack. Steam hissed. The brakeman checked the couplers between cars with his brakeman's club, and Mr. Marshall barked orders.

"All aboard!" the conductor shouted, and even though no one boarded and the whistle didn't blow, the train chugged away toward Raephy's new home.

Lucias Quintas
Cincinnatus Lamar

Engine #345 moved slower than a turtle in quicksand, and Raephy had swung the lantern back and forth, back and forth for what seemed like a thousand hours. She was certain her arm would drop off if she swung the lantern even one more time.

She had seen one cow on the tracks, but before anyone heard Raephy's warning, the brakeman chased the cow away with his club. Mr. Marshall didn't really need her help, and besides, the sky was showing the first signs of dawn. She blew out the flame, set the lantern on the floor, and rubbed her arms.

The workmen trudging beside the tracks were singing in rhythm with the slow *clack clack clack* of the

Engine #345 moved slower than a turtle in quicksand, and Raephy swung the lantern back and forth, back and forth.

wheels. "When Johnny Comes Marching Home Again, Hurrah! Hurrah!" Singing softly so she wouldn't bother her sisters, Raephy joined in. "The men will cheer, the boys will shout. The ladies they will all turn out—" She stopped when she realized they were singing different words. This wasn't a song about a Civil War soldier any more. It was about Mr. Black.

When Amos goes marching home again
Hurrah! Hurrah!
We'll give him a hearty farewell then
Hurrah! Hurrah!

The men will cheer, the boys will shout,
The ladies they will all turn out
And we'll all have a good laugh
When Amos goes marching home.

Too-too! Too-too-toot. The train whistle picked up the rhythm of the song, then sounded one very long loud ear-splitting blast and slowed to a stop. The conductor shouted. "This is it! The new home of Blackwell Station!"

"Sadie, Laura! We're home!" Raephy leaned as far out the window as she could. In the early white light of morning, she saw a broad level meadow stretched out on both sides of the tracks. On one side stood a large tent with a banner that read "Lamar Town Site Company."

"Town site!" Raephy's head whacked the windowsill. "Ouch!"

Mama ducked through the curtain, "What happened?"

"They're going to build us a town!"

"Yes, girls! We're going to build us a town! Now get dressed. Quickly! The men will unload the station, hook up the telegraph as fast as they can, then lay a siding switch for Engine #345. They have to clear the tracks for the other trains that will be coming."

Raephy scrambled into her clothes, raked her fingers through her hair, slipped down the stairwell and out the door toward the sound of a harmonica.

"Good morning, fuzzy head." Harry was sitting astride Sugar. "How was the ride?" He pushed back his cowboy hat with his thumb, a trait he'd picked up from the ranch hands.

"Long!" Raephy tiptoed across piles of lumber,

past the crates of chickens, and poised at the edge of the flatcar.

"Need a hand down?" Harry slipped his harmonica into a shirt pocket.

"Nope!" Raephy flew through the air and landed on both feet. "I'm going to look around."

"Spy a little?

"You bet!"

"Urf?" Jinx jumped up on her leg.

"Yes, you can go, too," she said, "You don't want to stay behind, do you?" She grabbed his cheeks and shook his head "no."

"Come on, Raephy, I'll give you a ride."

"Raephy McDowell!" Mama called from upstairs. "Where are you? I don't want you running around out there alone."

"It's all right, Mother." Harry cupped his hand to his mouth. "She's with me."

Harry grabbed Raephy's arm and helped her up behind the saddle. "Nice site, huh?" Harry said over his shoulder. "See those big cottonwoods by the river? Fishing will be great. Arrowhead hunting, too." He clicked his tongue, and Sugar stepped out into the meadow. "Look at the prairie dog holes. Hundreds of them. Careful, Sugar. Watch your step." He leaned forward, reining Sugar around the prairie dog mounds toward a village of small tents and into the welcoming aroma of food.

Raephy couldn't see everything fast enough. Where had all these people come from? Then suddenly she knew. They were homesteaders. She had no idea there were so many. Women were cooking and setting tables. Several men were hammering stakes into the ground, pacing and measuring, then hammering more stakes.

"See that fellow over there with the tripod?" Harry nodded with the brim of his hat. "He's a surveyor. He's measuring and marking where the streets will be. Streets and stores and houses and—"

"And a school?"

"Yup." Harry nodded and tipped his hat to a group of women who were laying out a huge meal on sawhorse tables. "Good morning, ladies." Enormous roasts of meat browned on a spit over an open fire, the juices sizzling in the flames. Steam from a gigantic, black-iron caldron puffed the delicious aroma of coffee into the air. One tent manned only by men offered nothing but kegs and

Harry balanced his plate as he nudged Sugar to a spot away from the stampede.

cups—the whiskey and beer those workers were talking about, Raephy bet.

With all the wonderful smells filling the air, it was no surprise that the workers unloaded the station much faster than they had loaded it. Engine #345 rolled onto a siding, bellowed a long, loud blast, and as the men stampeded toward the food, fiddles began to play the happiest music Raephy had ever heard.

"Here, child. Take this quickly before they get here." A woman with a big flowered apron dished up two steaming plates of food. "You must be McDowells. Welcome to your new home." She handed the plates up with a smile. "Come fall, I'll be living here, too. I'll be your new teacher."

"Really!" Raephy exclaimed. "And Harry's and Laura's and Sadie's, too?"

The teacher nodded.

"I can't wait to tell Laura! She loves school."

Harry balanced his plate as he nudged Sugar to a spot away from the stampede then helped Raephy down. They had just started to eat when Daddy, Laura, and Sadie joined them carrying plates heaped with food. "See that lady?" Raephy whispered, pointing with her eyes, not her finger. "She's our new teacher! And she's really nice."

"Anyone hungry besides me?" Daddy asked, taking a bite. "Ummm!"

Raephy was too busy eating to answer. She watched the sun rise on the workmen lined up at the tables and in front of the keg tent, and on people scattered by twos and threes over the whole town site. Some folks were putting up makeshift shacks or tents inside the freshly marked boundaries of their new property.

Raephy imagined the houses that would be there soon, a house on every lot, sunshine sparkling on the polished windows. She could almost hear children laughing and singing, and mothers calling, "Dorie, Sammy, Tom, come in now. It's time for bed!"

She would be invited for an overnight sleepover with her new friend, Kathleen. Yes. Kathleen would be her name, and she would call her "Kat", and they would be very best friends forever and ever. "I wish you were here now, Kat," she said.

Sadie's tickling fingers brought Raephy back to her senses. "Which cat?" Sadie teased. Harry and Laura were laughing at her, too.

"You're thinking out loud again, Raephy." Laura shook her head.

"Don't worry. I loaded all the cats on the train. But never again!" Harry rolled up a sleeve and held out his scratched arm. "Compared with cats, loading cattle is easy."

"Harry, if you're finished, take a plate to your mother, will you?" Daddy said. "Too bad she has to work today."

Raephy ate until she couldn't stand the thought of another bite. And then, with the sun beating down, the dancing began. Daddy danced with Raephy and Sadie, then Raephy and Sadie danced together. And Laura? Laura danced with the long string of men who lined up to ask her.

Six more trains arrived during the day carrying fresh workers who put the cattle chutes, chicken coop, and corrals back together. A crew dug a deep hole and covered it with a brand new two-seater outhouse. Blackwell Station looked almost the same as it had on Amos Black's ranch. Only better.

As the sun set over the new town, people were lying on the ground under tarps, in makeshift shacks, in wagons, and under wagon beds. A new town and people, people, people everywhere. The music of Harry's harmonica wafted up with the smoke from one of the campfires, but the rest of the family sprawled on the edge of the station platform looking out at the flickering lights. Even with all the excitement, Raephy couldn't keep her eyes from drooping. She leaned against Daddy and stroked Jinx's tummy as he lay on her lap with his paws up in the air.

"Daddy?"

"Yes, Raephy?"

"How will you get to the ranch every day? Will you ride the train? Will Harry have to leave Sugar out there?"

Daddy chuckled. "No. No, Raephy. I won't be going to the ranch any more."

"But what about—"

"Up to bed, everyone," Mama said, interrupting the thousand questions Raephy wanted to ask, especially about Mr. Black. "It's been a very long day."

"Get off, Jinx," Raephy leaned away as Daddy scooped Sadie into his arms. For a second Sadie's nose stopped whistling, then returned to its regular *tweet— tweet—tweet.*

"But this will still be Blackwell Station, won't it?"

"No," Mama said, herding Raephy toward the door. "It has a new name."

"But if it's not Blackwell Station," Raephy moaned, "we won't be special any more."

"Raephy, don't be silly!" Mama nudged her. "To bed!"

"What is it then?" Raephy asked. "What's the name of this new town?"

Daddy paused in the doorway. "It's official. The town site papers were signed in Washington. Our town will be named after Lucias Quintas Cincinnatus Lamar, the United States Secretary of the Interior."

"Eeuuuu! That's a terrible name! Lucias Quintas Cincinnatus Lamar? Why that? It's too long!"

Mama pivoted to Raephy, hands on hips. "You and your curious mind. This will be your last question for tonight. Agreed?"

Raephy nodded. "Agreed."

"All right," Mama said, all business-like. "This is a little complicated, so see if you can follow. Mr. I. R. Holmes is a land boomer. He makes towns. As the railroads came west, he built Garden City and many other railroad towns in western Kansas. Now he's moving into eastern Colorado to promote our town.

"Mr. Holmes convinced us to choose *Lamar* because the Secretary of the Interior decides where land offices and post offices and railroad stations will be. See?"

"Ha!" It was complicated, but Raephy saw. "So Mr. Lamar will feel all puffed up and important. Then he'll choose our town for all those things, right? Because we've named our town after him."

"Right." Daddy whispered over Sadie's tweety-snores. "Especially now that the railroad station is here."

"Tricky!" Raephy said. "Mr. Holmes must really be smart."

"I suspect he is." Daddy chuckled. "Tricky and smart. Like a politician. Having Lamar chosen for the railroad and post office would make it a good choice for the county seat, too. And a fine place to raise a family." He yawned. "Now, scoot! Go up to bed."

"What's a county seat?"

The only answer was a pat her own seat nudging Raephy in the door.

Mama lit a lantern and led the way upstairs. Daddy shifted Sadie higher onto his shoulder and followed, but

Laura lagged behind.

"I'll be up in a minute, Mama."

Suddenly Raephy was not so sleepy anymore. She hung back hiding beside the platform door.

"Miss McDowell?" A man's soft voice floated in from the darkness.

"Over here, Mr. Gobin," Laura whispered. "You'll be just fine under the platform tonight, William," Laura said. "It's one of my sister's favorite hideouts."

"I appreciate thy kindness, Miss McDowell, and I...I...I did so very much enjoy dancing with thee today."

Raephy peeked around the door frame to see this person with the unusual way of speaking. In the dim moonlight, she could see William Gobin open a toolbox and pull out a blanket. He should have a better place to sleep than under the platform, Raephy thought, like inside the station. But she couldn't say anything without being caught.

"Good night, William," Laura whispered. "Sleep well. Perhaps I shall see you, —thee— perhaps we shall see each other tomorrow."

Raephy scurried upstairs faster than a mouse, and fully dressed, snuggled under the covers next to Sadie, squeezed her eyes closed, opened her mouth, and see-sawed her way into a raucous snore. She didn't know if she fooled Laura or not. After one or two snorts, she was fast asleep.

Mr. Black

In the one-day-old town of Lamar, Colorado, the McDowell rooster knew exactly what to do. At his first "Cock-a-doodle-do!" Raephy scrambled out of bed and tiptoed downstairs to watch Mr. William Gobin crawl out from under the platform. Even rumpled from the night's sleep and trailing a few cobwebs, he was handsome. And just the right age for Laura.

Raephy thought Mama would insist on getting back into the usual Monday routine, and Raephy dreaded being stuck at the telegraph half the day OS–ing trains and learning spelling words. Raephy's first surprise of the morning was that she was wrong.

After breakfast, Mama tied a sunbonnet over her bun and said, "Come on, girls. Let's go spying." She winked at Raephy. "I mean visiting. Let's meet our new neighbors. Daddy's going to watch the telegraph for awhile."

Raephy charged ahead, then stopped to wait for Mama and her sisters to catch up. "Laura?" she said, peering at the flushed pink face of a smiling young woman. "Is that you?"

"Of course it's me, silly!" Laura spun in a little circle, twirling a lace parasol that Raephy had seen when she was snooping in Mama's big trunk. Stepping lightly, Laura grabbed Sadie's hand, and swinging her arm to the rhythm of the song Laura began to sing.

Did you ever hear tell of Sweet Betsy from Pike,
Who crossed the wide mountains with her lover Ike.

Today even more tents offering food and drink spread across the meadow. The whole town smelled of bacon. A large tent boasted a sign "HOTEL" and a fluttering flag "Open for Business."

"Good morning," Mama said to the hotel owner, who looked well scrubbed and well fed. "I'm Mrs. John

McDowell and these are my daughters, Laura, Raephy, and Sadie."

"Ah, yes! And I'm Fred W. Burger." He bowed slightly. "I understand we'll soon be neighbors." He gestured to the tent. "Of course, this is only temporary. I'll have a fine hotel standing here in six weeks, and that's a promise."

"I know someone who needs a place to stay!" The words tumbled out before Raephy had a chance to think. She held her breath, but it was too late.

"And who might that be?" Mr. Burger leaned forward, his eyebrows arched high.

"Ah—ah—" Raephy stood stiffly, wishing Laura away, then answered at telegraph speed, "AcarpenternamedWilliamGobin."

"Raephy McDowell! You little spy!"

"Laura, dear," Mama interrupted, speaking a little louder than necessary, "would you go take over for Daddy at the desk? After the next train arrives, there will be one more coming from Pueblo. It will be the last train today, so after you send the O.S., come find us again."

Avoiding eye contact with Raephy, Laura glanced around the crowd, smiled, then leaned toward Mama, nodded toward someone and whispered in Mama's ear. Try as she might, Raephy couldn't catch a word, but she did hear part of Mama's answer "...introduce him to Daddy, and keep Sadie with you."

Raephy watched Laura and Sadie, hand in hand, skip toward a young man who still had a tangle of cobwebs and leaves stuck to his back.

Raephy tugged on her mother's arm. "Look! There's another tent going up! It's grander than all the rest. Bye, Mr. Burger."

Long poles lifted the canvas that snapped in the faint breeze, but the tent rose quickly topped by a banner with the words "First Sale Town Lots Today." A board shaped like a thermometer stood at one side of the tent. An empty tripod stood at the other.

Raephy's head was spinning in the swirl of so many voices when a long piercing whistle silenced everyone. The most beautiful passenger train Raephy had ever seen approached and slowed gently to a stop.

The train was filled with people dressed as if they were going to an opera. Fancy hats with feathers fluttered out the windows. Handkerchiefs waved. Banners with gilded letters decorated the outside wooden panels of the coach cars. "Excursion Train" "I. R. Holmes Excursion Train, Garden City to Lamar." "Lamar, future 'Mascot City of the Plains.'"

Before Raephy could ask, 'What's a mascot?', the fiddlers reappeared, plunking their strings. Then pulling their bows and raising their voices, they began,

Home, home on the range
Where the deer and the antelope play,
Where never is heard a discouraging word....

"Look at all this!" Mama sat on the ground beside Raephy. "I knew they were bringing people in, but I had no idea there would be so many!"

Mr. Tall Man leapt from the train and ran into the station. "Mama!" Raephy pointed.

"It's all right." Mama smiled. "Daddy knows the combination."

In only the time it must have taken to open the safe, Mr. Tall Man ran out carrying the mysterious long roll of paper. He fastened the paper which was marked with little squares and numbers to the tripod.

"That's the town plat," Mama whispered, "a map

of streets and lots. Daddy and I already had a chance to see it when we—" Then she seemed to forget what she started to say.

Mr. Tall Man waved toward the train and a second man stepped down. Raephy guessed he must be Mr. I. R. Holmes himself because he looked so puffed up and important. Another man followed, carrying a funny-looking cone.

"Step right up!" the third man hollered through the cone. "All you home seekers and speculators. All you platters and boomers," he shouted, "step right up! Get your very own 'home on the range'. The first sale of town lots will commence in five minutes!"

The auctioneer set the cone aside. Passengers in their fancy clothes and homesteaders in calico and denim gathered round, and the rapid-fire prattle of the auctioneer began. Captain Cooper bustled among the newcomers with Mr. Ament, the young man from the handcar, at his heels.

"Do I hear…?" " Who'll raise it to….?" "Going…going…gone! Sold to the gentleman with the feather in his hatband!"

Young Mr. Ament was the very first to buy a lot. With each sale, Mr. Tall Man marked the thermometer with a rising column of red. $500, $1000, $1250.

"Remember, ladies and gentlemen," the auctioneer said at a normal speed, "your train ticket is free, absolutely free, when you purchase your lot today." Then he burst into the auctioneer talk that sped by even faster than the *dah-dit*s of Morse Code.

By five o'clock, the number beside the red line on the thermometer had risen to $45,000. "Imagine!" Mama exclaimed. "Forty-five thousand dollars in lots sold in a single day! We'll have so many new neighbors!"

"Who'llgivemefivehundredfivehundredfivehundred?" The auctioneer was pointing across the audience, when suddenly his hand dropped and his voice became quiet. "Thank you, ladies and gents. The sales tent is closed for the day. Be back tomorrow morning." Without another word, he ducked behind the sales tent and scurried away.

Tooo. Tooo. A train was pulling in from the west.

"Uh-oh! Hold on to your hat," Mama said, standing slowly and brushing grass from her skirt.

"I don't have my hat," Raephy said, walking beside Mama toward the arriving train. "Here comes Daddy!"

Her father strode across the clearing with Sadie and Laura sprinting to keep up. He spoke to Mama as if the rest of them weren't there. "Well, Emily. This is it. Let's hope for the best. Girls," he said quietly, "stay right here with us."

The familiar *clickity-clack clickity-clack* of wheels slowed, the brakes squealed, and the engine thunked to a stop.

The fiddlers stopped fiddling. The whole meadow of people became as quiet as Harry's sleeping turtle.

Mr. Amos Black stepped off the train, a small tremor rippled through the crowd.

Mr. Amos Black looked at the station. He looked at the corrals. He looked at the fences and cattle chutes. He looked at the tents and people, took off his hat, shook his head, then looked again. Slowly, his face changed from surprise to disbelief, then hardened into something cold and very very angry.

"Who did this?" he roared. "Who stole my station?" No one answered.

He slammed his hat back on. His lips disappeared into his black beard. His dark eyes narrowed. Then he drew the six-shooter from the holster at his side and swept it across the crowd.

"This is MY station!" he shouted. "I want to know

who ordered my station to be moved!" He leveled the six-shooter at Mr. Marshall, then at the Tall Man, then at Captain Cooper.

No one answered.

Raephy held her breath, remembering the telegram. *"Which of us will take it?"* Mama had asked. *"When he figures out what's happened, he'll be suspicious. He'll think the messenger is in on it."*

"Who!" Black yelled, slowing sweeping his gun toward Mama. "Who is responsible for this, Emily?"

Until she heard her own voice, Raephy didn't know what she was about to do. "You." The sound that came from her throat was barely a squeak. She tried again, "You are."

"Who said that?"

"Me." Raephy said, trembling from the tip of her toes to the top sprigs of her barbed wire hair. Suddenly, her feet flew off the ground, and Daddy's strong arm pinned her behind him, pressing her face into his stiff leather belt. She wiggled to one side, peeked out from beneath his elbow, and sucked in a deep shaky breath. "Blackwell Station got moved because of you, Mr. Black."

"You!" He glowered at Raephy. "You delivered that fake telegram! You know who sent it, don't you?" The holes in the barrel of Mr. Black's gun looked like the black eyes of a toad ready to jump.

"No," Raephy squeaked.

"Amos?" Daddy said in a low calm voice. "Do you realize you are pointing your gun at a child?"

Mr. Black jerked as if he'd been splashed by icy water. With a killer look at her parents, he slammed his six-shooter into its holster and narrowed his eyes at the cowering crowd. "You moved my station, but I'll move it back!" He flipped his hand toward the tired looking building. "This will always be Blackwell Station!"

Mr. Tall Man stepped forward. "No, Amos, it won't. Blackwell Station has a new name now—Lamar—same as this new town."

"Lamar? Lamar!" Mr. Black sputtered. "That's a terrible name. Way you've been hiding behind Raephy's skirts, you ought to name it after her."

He stuffed his thumbs under his belt, pivoted, and marched down the tracks. "I'll get my station back," he yelled over his shoulder, "and I'll get back at you, too. All of you!"

The workmen who'd walked the three miles from Black's ranch didn't start singing until Mr. Amos R. Black was out of earshot. One by one, as people understood the words, nervous laughter rippled through the crowd, then grew louder as everyone joined in.

When Amos goes marching home again
Hurrah! Hurrah!
We'll give him a hearty farewell then
Hurrah! Hurrah!

The fiddlers, then Harry's harmonica picked up the tune, but Raephy didn't feel like singing. She walked away from the crowd and stood alone.

The men will cheer, the boys will shout,
The ladies they will all turn out
And we'll all have a good laugh
When Amos goes marching home.

Mama and Daddy had followed her. They weren't singing, either. "It's just too bad," Daddy said. "Amos and I have known each other for a long time."

"Daddy, can he really get the station back?"

"Not likely."

Raephy turned to the long parallel set of railroad tracks, watching Mr. Black's figure shrink to a little black dot on the flat prairie. "I'm sorry for him, though. I felt like that when I had to miss dessert and go to bed alone." Mama's hand caressed her hair.

"Mama? Daddy?" Raephy said, "Having something named after you—like Blackwell Station—isn't really so special after all, is it?"

"No, Raephy, it isn't. Special comes from in here." Mama's finger wiggled against Raephy's chest. "But that's enough of all this long-faced talk." Mama looked at Daddy and smiled. "Speaking of special—"

That look! It was a look Raephy'd seen many times. A look that hid a secret. "What? Tell me!"

But Mama didn't answer. "Sadie," she called, "Laura, come join us. We have some special news."

Mama said quietly into Raephy's ear. "From all your spying Daddy and I thought you might have already figured it out."

"Figured what out?"

Mama's eyebrows raised and with a grin, she

shrugged.

"Come this way." Daddy stepped away from the railroad tracks toward the markers on the ground. He walked a straight line, turned forty-five degrees, and walked another straight line. "This is it, isn't it, Emily?" Mama nodded.

"Girls," he said, pointing to two rows of stakes in the ground. "This is First Street." He stepped over the stakes into a large square lot marked with string. "And our new house will be right here."

Raephy's ears buzzed. Her head spun. "Oh!" she could finally say. "Oh."

"Honest?"

"Really?"

"A house!"

"Our house!"

"Yes, my darling daughters!" Mama spun in a circle. "A home of our very own. And I, for one, plan to live here forever."

"A big house?" Sadie tugged on Daddy's arm.

Laura clasped her hands as if in prayer. "Will I have a room of my own?"

"Yes and yes!" Daddy swooped Sadie high into the

air. "Two stories. A stone house with gables and lots of rooms!" He put Sadie down, stood extra tall, and cleared his throat. "I have another surprise."

Raephy looked up at Daddy's sparkling eyes and knew that whatever he was about to say would be good. "As of today, your mother is not the only member of the McDowell family working for the Atchison, Topeka, and Santa Fe Railway."

"You, too, Daddy?" Raephy exclaimed.

Daddy swept the Stetson from his head and bowed. "Yes, ma'am. Me, too."

"Well, I never!" Raephy was trying to sort out everything that had happened. "So all those people who came to Blackwell Station—Mr. Marshall, the Tall Man, Captain Cooper, Mr. Ament. And that roll of paper, and the telegram? You and Mama are spies!"

"Oh, no!" Mama and Daddy laughed. "Daddy and I aren't spies, but we have been keeping lots of secrets for the Santa Fe. After we saw that Mr. Black was never going to agree to a town we had to make a choice, and we chose what was best for our family."

Raephy looked out across the meadow at the tired-looking Blackwell Station tilting on the skids. Then she let her eyes caress the town site where her future lay waiting. Everything she had ever wished for was coming true, just like in a fairy tale, and soon she'd have a whole town to spy on.

"But…I don't think I'll spy any more," Raephy decided. "I'll be too busy with school and parties and playing with all my friends. And keeping a whole bunch of new secrets."

The End

SWEET BETSY FROM PIKE

SIMPLY

Oh, don't you re-mem-ber sweet Bet-sy from Pike, Who crossed the wide prair-ies with her lov-er Ike, With two yoke of cat-tle and one spot-ted hog, A— tall shang-hai roost-er, an old yal-ler dog? *Chorus* Sing too-ral-i-oo-ral-i-oo-ral-i-ay.

They swam the wide rivers and crossed the tall peaks,
And camped on the prairie for weeks upon weeks.
Starvation and cholera and hard work and slaughter,
They reached California spite of hell and high water.
CHORUS: Sing too-ral-i-oo-ral-i-ay

They soon reached the desert, where Betsy gave out,
And down in the sand she lay rolling about;
While Ike in great terror looked on in surprise,
Saying, "Betsy, get up, you'll get sand in your eyes."
CHORUS: Sing too-ral-i-oo-ral-i-ay

WHEN JOHNNY COMES MARCHING HOME

LIVELY, VIGOROUS RHYTHM

When John-ny comes march-ing home a-gain Hur-rah!__ Hur-rah!__ We'll

give him a hear-ty wel-come then, Hur-rah!__ Hur-rah!__ The

men will cheer,__ the boys will shout, The lad-ies they__ will

all turn out, And we'll all feel gay When Johnny comes march-ing home.__

The old church bell will peal with joy, Hurrah! Hurrah!
To welcome home our darling boy, Hurrah! Hurrah!
The village lads and lassies say
With roses they will strew the way, And we'll all feel gay
When Johnny comes marching home.

Get ready for the Jubilee, Hurrah! Hurrah!
We'll give the hero three times three, Hurrah! Hurrah!
The laurel wreath is ready now
To place upon his loyal brow, And we'll all feel gay
When Johnny comes marching home.

In eighteen hundred and sixty-one, Hurrah! Hurrah!
That was when the war begun, Hurrah! Hurrah!
In eighteen hundred and sixty-two
Both sides were falling to, And we'll all drink stone wine
When Johnny comes marching home.

87

The Midnight Ride of Blackwell Station

is based on the true story of the "booming" of Lamar, Colorado. At midnight on May 22, 1886, Santa Fe Railroad Engine #345 pulled into Blackwell Station with empty flatcars and work cars filled with men. The workers, hired for $10, dinner, and all the beer and whiskey they could drink, loaded the two-story station onto the flatcars then walked three or four miles holding the load to keep it from falling off. The workers unloaded the station, reconnected the telegraph lines, and by the second day, land sales had begun.

Raephy McDowell and her family, Amos Black, Captain Cooper, and all others named in the story were real people. Their personalities, conversations, and the details of the roles they played in the events are creations of the author.

Acknowledgments

The author wishes to thank the following persons:

Edward Hawkins "Ted" Applegate III, Raephy's grandson, for McDowell family memories, insights, and photographs.

Thomas Jepsen, author of "Women Telegraph Operators in the Civil War," for information, advice, and infinite patience in responding to questions on railroads and telegraphers of the 1800s.

Ava Betz, historian and author of *A Prowers County History*.

The staff of the Colorado Railroad Museum, Golden, Colorado, for research assistance and hands-on telegraph experience.

Curator Kathleen M. Scranton, Caro Hedge, and the volunteers of Big Timbers Museum, Lamar, Colorado, for providing archival accounts of the founding of the boomtown of Lamar. Special thanks to summer volunteer, Debbie Herrera. Had Debbie not opened the museum at high noon on a hot July day, this book would not have been written.

About the Author

Mary Peace Finley
was raised in the southeastern
Colorado town of Fowler on
the Atchison, Topeka, and
Santa Fe Railroad line, eighty
miles west of Lamar. The
haunting wail of train whistles
and the click of wheels wove
indelible patterns through her
childhood. Joe Peace, Mary's
father, was the local agent for
the Standard Oil Company.
His office sat across the street from the Fowler Railroad
Station. Enormous gasoline and diesel tanks crouched
like huge headless monsters on metal legs next to the
tracks, a constant fire danger for Mary's dad and for the
town. "Just one spark—"

A pigtailed girl in a cowboy hat, Mary loved riding
with her dad to deliver fuel to outlying ranches. "Want
to ride out south with me tomorrow, Snooks?" her dad
would ask, "Out to the Red Top?" It meant leaving at
5:00 a.m. and bouncing for hours over dusty washboard
roads in the red Standard Oil truck following a night that
held more excitement than sleep.

The Dobbins were friends who worked for the railroad
and lived in a railroad car. When they rolled into town,

Mary's family was invited to "Come on over!" for dinner in their train car home. The car was like a real house, only long and narrow and everything inside seemed small.

Mary has written four other historical novels set in southeastern Colorado and along the Santa Fe Trail in 1845-1849. Four decades passed between the setting of those stories and 1886 when Blackwell Station rode into Lamar at midnight. By then, wagons were being replaced by trains and wheel ruts by railroad tracks.

Trains still ride the rails along the old Santa Fe Trail. The haunting wail of whistles and the click of wheels echo across the prairie, evoking memories and linking our lives to what has come before.

Contact Mary through her website:
www.MaryPeaceFinley.com
